Big
or
Little?

Fourteenth printing, March 2000

Annick Press Ltd.

We acknowledge the support of the Canada Council for the Arts,
the Ontario Arts Council, and the Government of Canada through
the Book Publishing Industry Development Program (BPIDP) for
our publishing activities.

Cataloguing in Publication Data
　Stinson, Kathy.
　　Big or little?

(Annick toddler series)
ISBN 0-920236-30-8 (bound). – ISBN 0-920236-32-4 (pbk.)

I. Lewis, Robin Baird. II. Title. III. Series

PS8587.T56B54　jC813'.54　C83-094034-0
PZ7.S74Bi

Distributed in Canada by:　　Published in the U.S.A. by Annick Press (U.S.) Ltd.
Firefly Books Ltd.　　　　　Distributed in the U.S.A. by:
3680 Victoria Park Avenue　Firefly Books (U.S.) Inc.
Willowdale, ON　　　　　　P.O. Box 1338
M2H 3K1　　　　　　　　　Ellicott Station
　　　　　　　　　　　　　　Buffalo, NY 14205

Printed and bound in Canada by
Friesens, Altona, Manitoba.

visit us at: **www.annickpress.com**

Big
or
Little?

**Story
Kathy Stinson**

**Art
Robin Baird Lewis**

Annick Press Ltd.
Toronto • New York • Vancouver

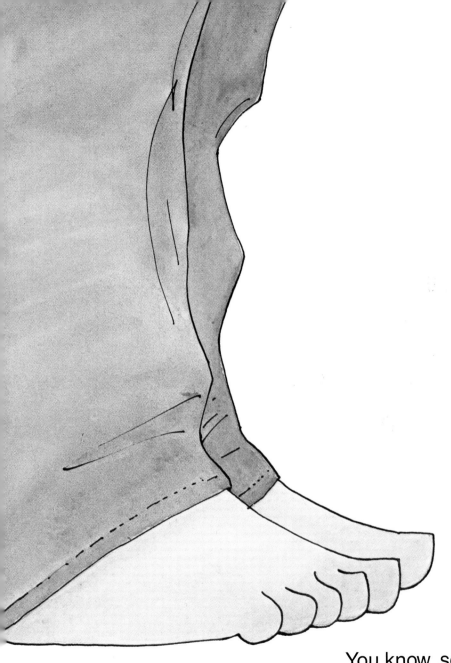

You know, sometimes I feel so big.

When I can tie my shoes,

and zip my jeans

and button my shirt all by myself,
that means I'm big.

But sometimes I feel so little.

When I can't   reach the button when I go and visit my friend,

that means I'm little.

When I remember to bring my library book back to school because it's Tuesday,

that means I'm big.

When my mom yells at me 'cause
I can't find my other sock, again,

that means I'm little.

When I make my own breakfast
before anyone else gets up,

that means I'm big.

Once in awhile I wake up and my
bed's wet, and that means I'm little.

When I help take care of my little sister,
that means I'm big.

When I have to sit in the chair because
I forgot and rode my bike out into the street,

that means I'm little.

When somebody says, "Thank you for holding the door, Matthew. That was very thoughtful," that means I'm big.

When I get lost between the bacon and the raisin bread, that means I'm little.

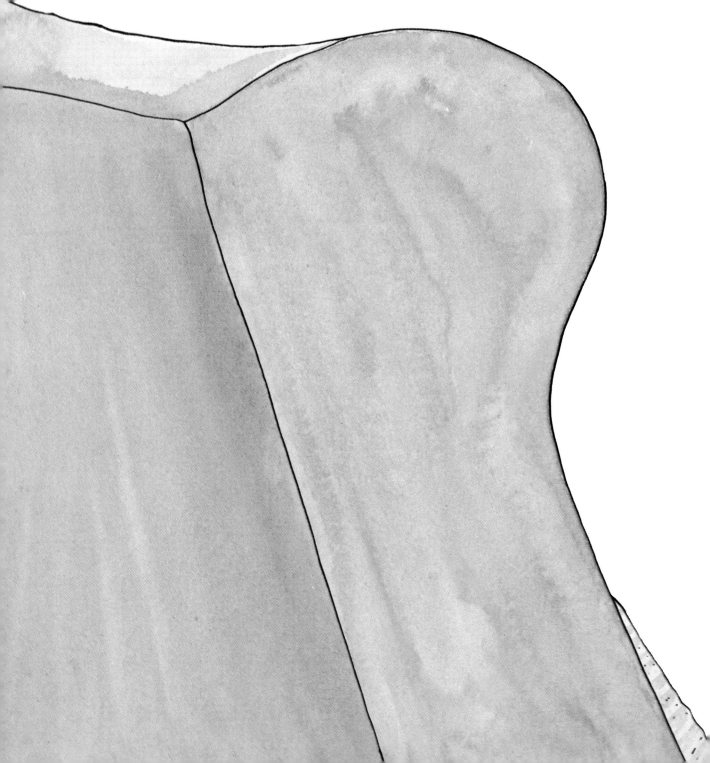

When my dad and I talk about space,
that means I'm big.

When my aunt buys me bunny pyjamas,

that means I'm little.

But when the bunny pyjamas don't come in my size,

that means I'm big.

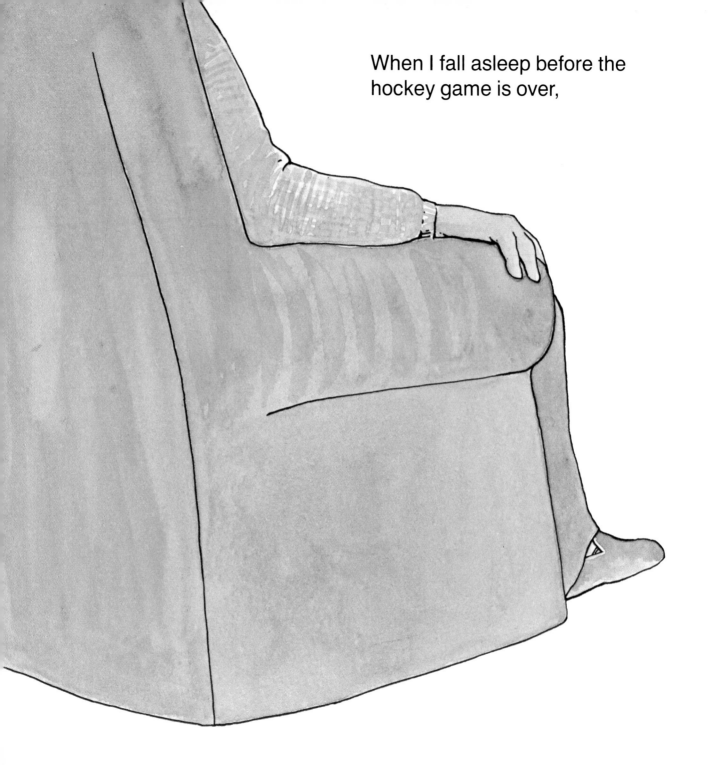

When I fall asleep before the hockey game is over,

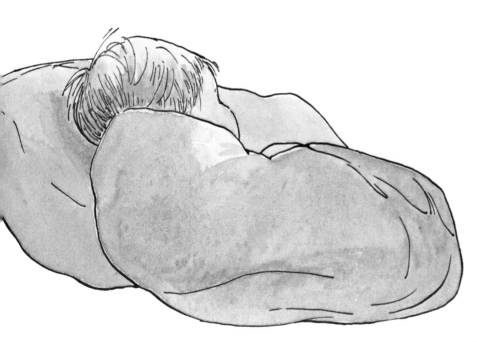

that means I'm little.

Then my dad lifts me up
in his big arms and
carries me up to bed.

Mostly I want to be big,
but sometimes being little
is pretty good too.

Other books by Kathy Stinson:

Red is Best
Mom and Dad Don't Live Together Any More
Those Green Things
The Bare Naked Book
Teddy Rabbit
The Dressed Up Book